P9-BYH-471

Camilla
the Cupcake Fairy

Tim Bugbird · Lara Ede

make
believe
ideas

Camilla

On Camilla's fifth birthday,
the Pink Fairy Post
sent to Camilla what she
dreamed of most.

Not a hat, or a doll, or a plant in a pot,
or anything else she'd already got.

She **tore** off the paper and **giggled** with glee.

"A **wand!**" cried Camilla.

"And meant just for **me!**"

It was so very shiny and sparkly and new.

Her very first wand! But **what** would it **do**?

If she waved it carefully
and closed her eyes tight,

could she wish for a **party** with **dancing** all night?

Or if she sat nicely,
not making a noise,
would it make her bed neatly
and put away toys?
Camilla
a
b
c
d

Or would it put on a **show**
with a **dancing** dog,

cartwheeling cats,
and a
singing frog?

The answer was **no**!

But what it would make,

Camilla was told, was

frosting for cake!

So she found a plain **cupcake**,

which she placed by her feet,

her **wand** at the ready,

to make a pink treat!

And holding the wand, Camilla stood straight.

She took a deep breath

but just could

not

wait . . .

She waved it so fast,

the wand would not stop

whirling and twirling

and flashing on top!

It jumped and it jerked,

with a rattle and a shake,

it jiggled and it juddered

'til she thought

it would break!

Then, with a BANG,

bright stars filled the air.

She looked for

sweet frosting,

but the cupcake was bare!

And there on the top,

not making a sound,

was a tiny white

mouse,

with eyes bright

and round!

So she started again, this time **taking care** to wave the wand gently. But look what was there!

Covering the cake where the frosting should be . . .

mashed potato was all she could see!

So she tried one more **wave**, not too **fast** or too **slow**.

Now topping the cake there was nothing but . . . **snow!**

Well, snowballs and snowmen
she didn't much mind,
but this fancy frosting
was just the
wrong kind!

"Oh dear," thought Camilla.
"This just isn't right.
My wand is not working.
I'll be here all night!"

But then, when it seemed she was down on her luck,

Ms. Sprinkles drove by in her pink fairy truck.

Camilla asked nicely, "What should I do?"

Her teacher said kindly, "I'll give you a clue!"

"Working alone is never much fun,
but with help from your friends, the job is soon done!"

So she called her friends on her pink fairy phone.

Molly and Maya were glad to be home.

Said Molly to Maya,
"Our friend's in a state!
Let's fly to Camilla,
this problem
won't wait!"

They held the **wand** steady
with eyes closed *tight*.

As they worked hard together,
it shone a **bright** light.

Then crossing their fingers
in a shower of gold **twinkles**,
they all **wished** together
for frosting and
sprinkles!

All of a sudden,
the fairy friends found
the tastiest treat,
just there on the ground.
With sparkling
sprinkles
and frosting
so sweet,
the best-ever
cupcake
was right at their feet!

So the wand could work wonders, but nothing compared
to the gift of true friendship the three fairies shared!